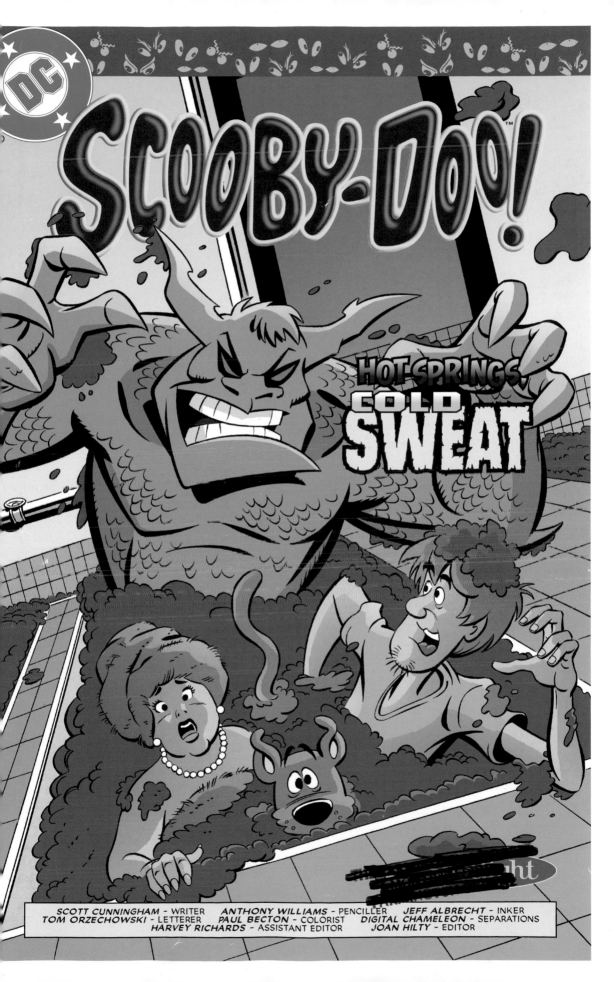

SCOOBY-DOO!

HOT-SPRINGS, COLD SWEAT

SCOTT CUNNINGHAM - WRITER   ANTHONY WILLIAMS - PENCILLER   JEFF ALBRECHT - INKER
TOM ORZECHOWSKI - LETTERER   PAUL BECTON - COLORIST   DIGITAL CHAMELEON - SEPARATIONS
HARVEY RICHARDS - ASSISTANT EDITOR   JOAN HILTY - EDITOR

VISIT US AT
www.abdopublishing.com

Reinforced library bound edition published in 2010 by Spotlight, a division of the ABDO Group, 8000 West 78th Street, Edina, Minnesota 55439. Spotlight produces high-quality reinforced library bound editions for schools and libraries. Published by agreement with Warner Bros.—A Time Warner Company. All rights reserved. Used under authorization.

Printed in the United States of America, Melrose Park, Illinois.
092009
012010

 PRINTED ON RECYCLED PAPER

Library of Congress Cataloging-in-Publication Data

Cunningham, Scott.
  Scooby-Doo in Hot springs, cold sweat / writer, Scott Cunningham ; penciller, Anthony Williams ; inker, Jeff Albrecht ; colorist, Paul Becton ; letterer, Tom Orzechowski. -- Reinforced library bound ed.
     p. cm. -- (Scooby-Doo graphic novels)
  ISBN 978-1-59961-695-7
  1. Graphic novels. I. Williams, Anthony, 1964- II. Scooby-Doo (Television program) III. Title. IV. Title: Hot springs, cold sweat.
  PZ7.7.C86Sc 2010
  741.5'973--dc22

                                 2009032900

All Spotlight books have reinforced library bindings and
are manufactured in the United States of America.

STEAM ROOM

"THERE'VE BEEN HALF A DOZEN ACCIDENTS IN THE LAST TWO WEEKS."

EXCUSE ME-- WHAT'S THIS?

"AT FIRST, THEY WERE JUST LITTLE THINGS..."

WHY IS THIS DOOR LOCKED?! I DEMAND TO KNOW!

rattle rattle

"ACCIDENTS... MISHAPS... STRANGE OCCURRENCES...

"BUT THESE LAST COUPLE... THEY WERE VERY CLOSE..."

OH NO!

"FRANKLY, THINGS GOT SCARY!"

POP

POP

HISSSSSSS

"THEN THEY GOT SCARIER..."

YIAAHH!!

BAM!

BAM!

BAM!

HSSSSSS

HOT SPRINGS, COLD SWEAT

SCOTT CUNNINGHAM - WRITER   ANTHONY WILLIAMS - PENCILLER   JEFF ALBRECHT - INKER
TOM ORZECHOWSKI - LETTERER   PAUL BECTON - COLORIST   DIGITAL CHAMELEON - SEPARATIONS
HARVEY RICHARDS - ASSISTANT EDITOR   JOAN HILTY - EDITOR

...ESPECIALLY AFTER *THIS!*

IT WAS SCRATCHED ON THE BACK OF ONE OF OUR TRAINER'S CLIPBOARDS, FOUND AT THE SCENE OF YESTERDAY'S UNFORTUNATE... *INCIDENT* IN THE WEIGHT ROOM.

A PICTO-GRAPH...

A DEVIL!

OR *DEMON,* MS...?

HOT SPRINGS HEALTH SPA

PLEASE, CALL ME *CRYSTAL.*

ANYWAY, SOME ACCIDENT VICTIMS SAY THEY SENSED AN *EVIL PRESENCE.*

the body temple FITNESS CENTER

the body temple

HOT SPRINGS HEALTH SPA

I'M SENSING AN "EVIL PRESENCE" *TOO.*

WHEN DID THAT UGLY THING GO UP?

TWO MONTHS AGO. AND THE COMPETITION IS *KILLING ME!*

IT'S *BIG.*

REAH.

BUT IT'S DEFINITELY *MISSING SOME-THING.*

LIKE, THIS SANDWICH IS JUST TOO *HEALTHY!*

THIS PLACE IS SO MACROBIOTIC, THEY *FRISKED* US BEFORE THEY LET US IN.

MAN, WE *AT LEAST* NEED TO *MELT* THE *TOFU CHEESE*-- THAT COULD JUNK UP THE SANDWICH A *LITTLE BIT!* THEY DON'T EVEN *COOK* THE FOOD!

RAW ROOD? RHAT R'RE RHEY... RANIMALS?!

THEY TOOK OUR *SCOOBY SNACKS!*

I'LL ARRANGE EVERYTHING... JUST *ENJOY.*

HEY! GANG!

LOOK. SOMEONE USED THEIR FINGER TO WRITE A MESSAGE ON THE STEAMED-UP GLASS!

AND A DRAWING. *THE* DRAWING!

WHAT?!

IT SAYS IT'S FROM THE *HOT SPRINGS DEMON.*

OH NO...THE *LEGENDS* ARE *TRUE!*

"*WHAT WAS PURE HAS NOW BEEN STAINED. LET BLOOD WASH IT CLEAN.*"

THE NATIVE AMERICANS WHO LIVED HERE A CENTURY AGO BELIEVED THE HOT SPRINGS WERE THE HOME OF A *GOD.*

THE SPA BUILDING HAS RUINED THE PURITY OF THE SPRINGS. SO THE *HOT SPRINGS DEMON* HAS RETURNED. I CAN'T IMAGINE ANYTHING *MORE* HORRIBLE!

UH, MS. FINE-- CRYSTAL-- I WONDER IF I COULDN'T HAVE A WORD WITH YOU.

the body temple

WELL, PERHAPS THERE *IS* ONE OTHER THING THAT'S *WORSE!*

PHISSHH

OH MY!!!

TYLER-- DARLING-- WHAT... WHAT ARE YOU DOING?!

WHY...*DARLING*... I'M TRYING TO DRIVE YOU *INSANE!* AS MANY THERAPISTS AS YOU SEE IN A *WEEK,* I DIDN'T THINK IT WOULD BE *SO HARD!*

BUT... BUT *WHY?*

BECAUSE I'M *SICK* OF WATCHING YOU *WASTE* YOUR *MONEY*-- MONEY *I'D* INHERIT IF ONLY I COULD HAVE YOU *INSTITUTIONALIZED!*

FACE IT-- YOU'LL *NEVER* BE A BIG STAR AGAIN! YOU'RE ALL *WASHED UP!*

NO-- *YOU'RE* THE ONE ALL WASHED UP, *MR. HARTLEY!*

YOU MEAN THE *EX*-MR. HARTLEY!

PISSHH

HEY MAN, THIS TIME IT'S A *GOOD* THING LIZ GOT *STEAMED!*

ROH, ROTHER!

THE END

YES, DETECTIVE NAKAJIMA. WE'VE SPOTTED HIM AT THE SCENES OF SEVERAL OF THE THEFTS.

LIKE, I SNAPPED THAT PICTURE OF HIM RIGHT WHEN HE ESCAPED FROM US AT THE INDIAN TEMPLE!

I WOULD HAVE ASKED HIM TO POSE, BUT HE SEEMED TO BE IN A HURRY. ⸗HEH-HEH⸗

HMMM. WE'LL PUT THIS PICTURE OUT TO ALL THE INTERNATIONAL LAW AGENCIES AND SEE IF WE CAN'T FIND OUT WHO HE IS.

IN THE MEANTIME, LET'S DISCUSS THE TWO RELEVANT GEM STONES WHICH HAVE NOT YET BEEN STOLEN.

ONE IS IN CHINA, WHERE IT IS BEING CAREFULLY GUARDED. THE OTHER, AS YOU KNOW, IS HERE IN TOKYO, OR RATHER...

... IT WAS.

YOU CAN'T MEAN...?

IT'S BEEN STOLEN? THEN WE ARE TOO LATE!

PLEASE... IT HAS NOT BEEN STOLEN. IT'S BEEN MOVED TO A SECRET LOCATION.

WHY ARE YOU SO CERTAIN THAT OUR STONE IS THE ONE WHICH THE THIEF WILL TRY TO STEAL NEXT, AND NOT THE ONE IN CHINA?

WELL, DETECTIVE... CALL IT A HUNCH.

THIS IS A PICTURE OF WHAT "**THE DRAGON'S EYE**" IS SAID TO LOOK LIKE WHEN ALL OF ITS PARTS ARE FITTED TOGETHER.

THE THIEF BEGAN WITH **THIS** PIECE IN FRANCE, THEN THESE ONES IN RUSSIA, ITALY, AND SYRIA.

THEY ALL FORM THE **FACETS** SURROUNDING THE "**PUPIL**" OF "THE DRAGON'S EYE."

THE ONLY FACET HE HADN'T TAKEN AT THAT POINT WAS THE ONE FORMED BY THE **TWO SACRED EARRINGS OF KALI.**

THAT'S HOW WE KNEW TO GO TO **INDIA**-- ONLY HE GOT THERE JUST AHEAD OF US.

AS YOU SAID, THERE ARE ONLY TWO PIECES LEFT-- THIS CROWN-LIKE PIECE AT THE BOTTOM, AND THE "PUPIL" ITSELF.

SYMBOLICALLY, THE PUPIL IS THE **CENTER** OF THE **EYE.** IT IS THE PART THAT LETS IN LIGHT--THE PART WE **SEE** WITH.

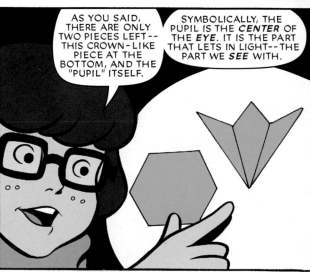

I WOULD THINK THAT THIS "FOCAL POINT" WOULD BE SAVED FOR **LAST.** THIS IS THE PIECE WHICH WILL HAVE THE IMPORTANT ROLE OF **COMPLETING** THE REASSEMBLED DRAGON'S EYE.

THE PUPIL IS **ALSO** THE PIECE LOCATED IN CHINA. MY FEELING IS THAT OUR THIEF IS CHINESE, BECAUSE THE DRAGON'S EYE SEEMS LIKE IT WOULD HAVE THE MOST IMPORTANCE TO SOMEONE FROM THE **SAME** CULTURE AS THE EYE ITSELF.

IF HE **IS** FROM THE CHINESE MAINLAND -- AND DIDN'T STEAL IT FIRST AS HE HEADED OUT TO STEAL ALL THE OTHER PIECES -- IT STANDS TO REASON THAT HE WILL STEAL IT WHEN HE RETURNS **HOME!**

THE DRAGON'S EYE IS REPUTED TO HAVE *GREAT POWER*...

...ENOUGH TO CONQUER THE *WORLD.*

"FOR ALL WE KNOW, THAT LEGEND MAY BE *TRUE.*"

thocka-thocka-thocka-thocka

ONE THING'S FOR SURE. IF OUR MYSTERY THIEF TRIES TO GET TO THE BOAT WAY OUT HERE, WE'LL SEE HIM COMING LONG BEFORE HE ARRIVES!

CAN YOU BELIEVE OUR LUCK, SCOOB? LIKE, IMAGINE THE KIND OF FOOD THAT GETS SERVED IN THE GALLEY OF A LUXURY YACHT!

ROODLES, REEF TERIYAKI, ROYSTERS...

YOU'RE BEING AWFULLY QUIET, MR TSUBURAYA. IS EVERYTHING OKAY?

YES, THANK YOU, VELMA-SAN. I DO NOT LIKE FLYING, SO IT TAKES A LOT OF *CONCENTRATION* FOR ME TO REMAIN CALM.

WE WILL HAVE PLENTY OF TIME TO TALK, ONCE WE ARE ABOARD THE BOAT.

SPEAKING OF THE BOAT, ISN'T THAT MR SATSUMA'S YACHT RIGHT BELOW US?

WHY ARE WE FLYING *PAST* IT?

BECAUSE THAT'S NOT OUR DESTINATION. THE SATSUMAS' YACHT IS A *DECOY,* MEANT TO DRAW THE THIEF INTO A TRAP.

OUR *REAL* DESTINATION IS...

"...A *FISHING BOAT* JUST A FEW MINUTES FURTHER OUT."

WELL, LOOK ON THE BRIGHT SIDE, YOU TWO.

WITH ALL THE FISH THIS BOAT CAN PULL IN, THERE'S BOUND TO BE MORE SUSHI THAN EVEN *YOU* CAN EAT!

YOU'VE GOT TO ADMIT, THIS WAS A CLEVER IDEA.

"THE TOWER" WILL BE SAFE ABOARD THIS UNSUSPICIOUS- LOOKING FISHING BOAT--

--WHILE THE THIEF STUMBLES INTO THE TRAP SET BY THE POLICE ABOARD THE SATSUMAS' YACHT.

MAYBE. BUT I WOULDN'T UNDERESTIMATE OUR THIEF.

HE'S FLYING INTO THE *HOLD* WHERE WE KEEP THE FISH!

THERE'S A *HATCH* IN THE HOLD THAT LEADS TO THE REST OF THE SHIP. HE'LL PROBABLY COME UP THE MAIN STAIRS!

HE'S AFTER "THE TOWER!"

IF WE HURRY, WE CAN TRAP HIM WITH THESE *NETS...*

NOT HERE!

ROT HRERE REITHER!

LIKE, THE WAY BACK UP TO THE DECK MUST BE HERE SOMEWHERE...

HOPEFULLY, WE'LL FIND THE *GALLEY* INSTEAD!

HE'S COME BACK OUT!

DON'T LET HIM GET AWAY!

Caw-Caw-Caw!

DUCK!

CLANG!

≳SNIFF
AH, SMELL THAT *FRESH SEA AIR!*

≳SNIFF
RAND FRESH FRISH!

GOOD WORK, SHAGGY AND SCOOBY!

WHAT'D WE MISS?

RUH?

LOOK, OUR TENGU WAS "FLYING" FROM A WIRE!

IT LEADS UP TO THAT *HELICOPTER!* THE PILOT'S CUTTING THE OTHER END LOOSE!

IT'S NOT OUR THIEF. JUST ANOTHER HIRED HAND!

LOOKS LIKE WE FINALLY WON A ROUND. WE CAPTURED HIM BEFORE HE GOT HIS HANDS ON "THE TOWER"!

THEN IT MUST STILL BE SAFE WITH MR. TSUBURAYA.

I...I'M SORRY.

WHAAAT??

I DID EVERYTHING I COULD, BUT THE TENGU FLEW INTO ME WITH SUCH *FORCE*, I WAS KNOCKED ACROSS THE CABIN.

BEFORE I COULD DO ANYTHING, HE PUT "THE TOWER" IN A CONTAINER, THREW IT OUT THE PORTHOLE...

...AND *FLEW BACK OUT OF THE ROOM!*

LATER...

WE HAVE NOT RECOVERED "THE TOWER," NOR HAVE WE FOUND THE MYSTERIOUS HELICOPTER, BUT...

WE DID FIND *THIS*-- A STRANGE *FLAG* THAT HAD BEEN SURREPTITIOUSLY RUN UP THE MAST SOMETIME LAST NIGHT!

THAT'S HOW THE TENGU THIEF KNEW IT WAS ON THE FISHING BOAT AND NOT ON THE SATSUMAS' YACHT!

THE THIEF HAD AN *ACCOMPLICE* ON THE FISHING BOAT, WHO RAN UP THE FLAG AS A SIGNAL TO THE COPTER!

MR. TSUBURAYA!

NONE OF THE PORTHOLES ON THAT BOAT *OPENED*-- AND THE TENGU *COULDN'T* HAVE "FLOWN" ALL THE WAY TO THE CABIN THAT CONTAINED "THE TOWER." HE WAS ATTACHED TO THAT WIRE!

ALL HE DID WAS DIVE INTO THE HOLD, WAIT, AND THEN GET TUGGED BACK OUT BY THE HELICOPTER!

OH, NO.

I JUST SAW HIM GOING INTO THE MEN'S WASH-ROOM -- HE SAID HE'D BE RIGHT WITH US!

A *DISGUISE!*

YOU WERE RIGHT--THIS THIEF OF YOURS IS A *MASTERMIND.* NOW, THERE IS ONLY *ONE* CHANCE LEFT TO APPREHEND HIM.

ONE LAST CHANCE IS ALL WE'LL *NEED.*

WE'LL GET TO THE HEART OF THE DRAGON'S EYE -- IN *CHINA!*

TO BE CONTINUED...